Beauty
and the Beast

Beauty
and the Beast

by
Madame le Prince
de Beaumont

Adapted by
Kathleen Rizzi

Illustrated by
Marcel Laverdet

Modern Publishing
A Division of Unisystems, Inc.
New York, New York 10022

Series UPC: 38200

Cover art by Bob Berry

Contents

Prologue 11

CHAPTER 1
Beauty 13

CHAPTER 2
The Merchant .17

CHAPTER 3
Beauty's Sisters 21

CHAPTER 4
A Letter Brings New Hope 25

CHAPTER 5
More Disappointments 29

CHAPTER 6
Lost in the Woods 35

CHAPTER 7
The Great Castle 39

CHAPTER 8
The Next Morning 45

CHAPTER 9
The Beast 51

CHAPTER 10
Treasures from the Castle 59

CHAPTER 11
A Bittersweet Reunion 63

CHAPTER 12
Beauty's Decision 69

CHAPTER 13
Beauty Goes to the Beast's Castle 77

CHAPTER 14
A Sad Farewell 87

CHAPTER 15
Beauty's Room 93

CHAPTER 16
Visions 99

CHAPTER 17
An Evening Together 105

CHAPTER 18
The First Proposal 111

CHAPTER 19
Encore 115

CHAPTER 20
Time Passes 123

CHAPTER 21
Shadows in the Moonlight 127

CHAPTER 22
The Magical Theater 131

CHAPTER 23
Beauty's Request 137

CHAPTER 24
A Family Reunion 141

CHAPTER 25
Envy Everlasting .149

CHAPTER 26
The Dream 153

CHAPTER 27
Searching for the Beast 157

CHAPTER 28
No Longer a Beast 163

CHAPTER 29
The Evil Fairy .169

CHAPTER 30
Reliving the Past 173

CHAPTER 31
A Wedding at the Great Hall 181

Epilogue 187

About the Author 189

Prologue

Deep in the woods, where fairies and sprites, imps and ogres still exert power over mortals, stands a castle. Unseen by passersby, the lonely castle remains silent except for the pitiful sighs of its forlorn master.

He no longer knows how long he has walked through the empty halls and grounds of his isolated estate. As time passes, he wanders alone and waits... and waits...and waits....

CHAPTER 1

Beauty

B eauty woke at dawn, as was her custom since coming to live in the country. Usually the first rays of the sun entering the small circular window of her room in the loft of the cottage woke her from her dreams. But today, it was the onset of winter's chill and the sound of her brothers yelling.

"Beauty, where is our breakfast?" Claude asked.

"We must get an early start today," Henri called up the stairs of the country home where the family had come to live this past year.

For a moment longer, Beauty lingered beneath the covers. In her dream, she and her family were well dressed and enjoying an elegant evening in town. Handsome suitors were competing for her sisters' attention. The youngest of the children, she was on her father's arm as they left the concert hall with her brothers trailing behind.

Beauty was only sixteen years of age. She had a good heart and a pleasant disposition and knew some things in life were beyond one's control. Unlike her sisters and brothers, Beauty met every day with a smile and a happy heart. What she couldn't change, she accepted and made the most of.

In fact, during the past year she had worked hard and found that both her physical strength and her character were none the worse for the experience.

Beauty had many friends and admirers, all of whom knew that her physical beauty was only a hint of the loveliness of her heart.

"I'm coming," she answered, throwing

the covers aside. She dressed quickly in a modest dress and apron. Then, after tying up her hair with a ribbon, she ran down the stairs to begin her daily routine of cooking and housekeeping.

CHAPTER 2

The Merchant

"Good morning, Father," Beauty said, hugging him. While his sons took their seats at the table, he looked up from the morning letters, smiled, and returned a warm hug acknowledging his favorite daughter's presence.

When Beauty's father had learned that his fortune was lost as a result of bad luck and dishonest clerks, he had moved his family from their town house to their country home more than one hundred miles away.

It upset his children greatly since they had to give up the lavish way of life that their father's wealth had afforded them. They had become accustomed to the very best that money could buy. Now that they were poor, Beauty and her siblings had to work the land and manage livestock for a living.

Beauty worked hard every day while her proud sisters grumbled and refused to lift a finger to help. Elise and Rene were very put out by the mere thought of having to work and live in the country. They taunted their little sister for having so cheerfully accepted what could not be changed.

"Look at our little Beauty," Elise would tease, "happy to be sweeping."

"Beauty, when you finish that chore, run and fetch my pillow," Rene demanded whenever Beauty had her hands full with dishes or laundry.

Beauty never complained about her sisters' mean behavior toward her, although she was often made to suffer by their cruel actions.

The decline in the family's status made Beauty's brothers sad, too, but

they grudgingly accepted their lot. Like their father, they were grateful for such a good-hearted sister.

The merchant knew that each of his children met the challenges that life brought them differently. He was grateful for Beauty's high spirits and hard work, but he did his best to ease the burdens that had come on the family as a result of his misfortune.

CHAPTER 3

Beauty's Sisters

Elise and Rene were not only jealous of Beauty's lovely features, but were angry because she was kind and sincere.

Beauty's sisters were known by all to be prideful and arrogant. During the days of the family's prosperity, when they lived in town in a lovely home with servants, they often shunned the company of the daughters and wives of other prosperous merchants, businessmen, and landowners, believing themselves to be better than everyone else.

They also scorned the advances of the most prosperous suitors, preferring to wait to marry a duke or an earl at the very least. They considered anyone untitled to be beneath them.

Although Elise and Rene treated their suitors badly, when their father lost his fortune, the haughty girls were certain that they could arrange a quick match and marry well.

But those suitors disappeared when they learned that the family was now poor. None of those fine gentlemen wanted to take a penniless, proud wife.

In fact, everyone who knew them believed that the mean-spirited sisters had finally gotten what they deserved.

While the neighbors secretly enjoyed Elise and Rene's hardship, they were heartbroken that Beauty suffered. The family's friends cared about Beauty's fate since she was a most wonderful and deserving person.

Elise and Rene hated Beauty now more than ever because Beauty's many suitors still wanted to marry her.

Beauty was consoled by her suitors' concern for her future, but she felt she was too young to marry. Instead, she chose to stay with her father to help him during this difficult time.

Her suitors graciously understood her decision, wished her well, and remained her dear friends.

A Letter Brings New Hope

Whilе Beauty was cleaning up after the morning meal, her father rose from his chair and waved a letter in the air.

"Good news has finally come!" he shouted. "One of the ships has arrived at last! I must go and see what I can get by selling the merchandise."

Wakened by the commotion, Elise and Rene came running down the steps in their nightgowns and robes.

"Oh, Father, we'll be rich again," Elise shouted.

"We can leave this dreadful house and move back to town," added Claude.

"We'll be rich gentlemen again," Henri said aloud dreamily.

"Father, bring us back new gowns and shoes and hats," demanded Rene.

"See if you can bring some jewelry, too, won't you?" asked Elise.

"I'll see what I can do," their father promised.

Beauty did not ask for anything. She wondered if the money her father would receive could ever be enough to satisfy her sisters.

Noticing how quiet she had become, he asked, "What do you want, Beauty?"

"Perhaps just a rose, which is so hard to find here," she said. If she didn't ask for something, she thought, it would make her sisters angry.

"I'll see what I can do," he said, touching her cheek tenderly. Then, with the help of his sons, he prepared for his journey to town to meet with his lawyer.

CHAPTER 5

More Disappointments

The seaside town was bustling with activity. Ships were docked and being loaded and unloaded by workmen and sailors. Merchants, tradesmen, and sailors were conducting their business, while townspeople and country folk milled about. Children ran through the streets between the horses and carts, grabbing on to their parents' hands so as not to get lost in the crowd.

When the merchant arrived, he went to see his lawyer.

"It is good to see you, sir," Beauty's father said, extending his hand to the lawyer. The man hardly looked up to acknowledge the merchant's presence.

"Good day to you," the lawyer muttered, frowning. "Although it won't be a day of good news for you, monsieur, I regret to say."

"What do you mean?" the merchant asked, taking the letter about his merchandise out of his pouch.

"The merchandise has finally arrived, but there is very little of it. It will be confiscated by creditors to whom you owe great sums of money," the lawyer responded. "It seems there is not enough

money to pay off your debts. You are poorer than before."

"How can this be?" the merchant cried in despair.

"Come and take a seat and see what I've found," said the lawyer.

The merchant and the lawyer carefully went over all of the accounts. The lawyer said that the bulk of the merchandise was lost at sea, and customs agents and profiteers had stolen much of the rest of it. The merchant owed more money than he ever imagined.

The merchant thanked the lawyer for his help, and turned to leave.

"I will, of course, inform you if anything changes, monsieur," the lawyer assured him.

The merchant left town with a heavy heart. He wondered how he would explain this new disappointment to his children.

He knew that Beauty would make the best of it. He looked forward to her

smiles and hugs upon his return. As for his other children, he knew that his sons would grumble but would be cheered by Beauty's good nature. His other daughters would be a problem, and he feared that they would take out their resentment on Beauty.

"What am I to do?" he whispered, looking skyward. He hoped that on the journey home he would find the courage to face his family.

CHAPTER 6

Lost in the Woods

Weary from traveling for days, the merchant was very close to home and was looking forward to seeing his children in spite of his bad news. Then he got lost in the forest.

How often I've traveled this road, he thought as he came to a crossroads. "I am certain this is the way," he mumbled, pulling his horse's reins with fingers that were becoming numb from the cold.

An hour or so later, it seemed he had come to the same crossroads. "This is not possible!" he said, sighing with growing frustration as he led the horse in the other direction this time.

As he rode on, the weather changed.

Snow and freezing rain fell mercilessly about him. The bitter cold made him shiver uncomfortably.

It was so windy that twice he fell off his horse, which continually lost its footing on the icy roads. Traveling was becoming more and more dangerous and the merchant more and more weary.

When night fell, he wondered whether he would freeze to death or be lost so long in the woods that he would starve. When he heard wolves howling, he feared being eaten by them.

"I am doomed," he said, sighing. Clutching his horse's reins and gathering his coat and hat about him, he rode on for hours through the icy mist and swirling winds.

Suddenly there was a break in the trees. The merchant could see a path through the forest. As he rode along the path, the weather changed again. It was no longer windy, snowing, and cold, but becoming pleasantly warm.

Ah, perhaps there is a place to rest nearby, he thought hopefully.

In the distance there was light. He rode toward it, still hoping to find shelter. Soon he reached a courtyard that bordered a magnificent estate with a castle and stables and other smaller buildings around them.

The merchant entered the courtyard. The area was thoroughly lit, but no one was there to receive him.

CHAPTER 7

The Great Castle

Seeing the stable door open, the merchant directed his horse into it. The starving horse began to eat all of the hay and oats it could find.

"Poor beast," the merchant said. "I hope the master here doesn't mind."

The merchant secured the horse in the stable and walked toward the main building. It was a large palace with turrets and gargoyles decorating gables that pointed toward the sky.

Numerous statues stood in the courtyard leading to the castle. They were lifesize and lifelike, scattered in no particular design. They were all the same pale color, but each was dressed differently. Some appeared to be soldiers, some servants, and others nobility. The merchant hurried on since he was still cold from his trip.

He approached the doors of the palace and entered cautiously. The large entranceway was decorated with tapestries, candelabra, and rich furnishings. A gilded mirror covered one of the walls. As he walked past the mirror, he saw something reflected in it.

"Hello," he called, turning around quickly, but he saw no one. When he looked into the mirror a second time, he could only see his own reflection—a red-cheeked, shivering, stooped man badly in need of a fire, food, and a place to rest.

"Is anyone here?" he called out. His words echoed throughout the hall. Since there was no answer, he walked on and found a welcoming fire burning in the fireplace of a comfortable sitting room. To his suprise, he saw a table set for one, spread with a bountiful meal.

Although he was starving, at first he didn't want to help himself to the meal. Perhaps someone will come while I get warm, he thought as he moved as close to the fire as possible.

Hours later, still no one had come into the sitting room. The merchant was amazed that the fire still roared, never lessening to embers in all that time. Unbearably hungry, he sat down and dined on delicious chicken and other roasted meats. He enjoyed fresh fruits, sweets, and refreshing cool water. As he ate, he noticed how elegant everything in the palace was.

Why doesn't someone come? he wondered. He crossed the hall and entered several smaller apartments. Each apartment had exquisite furnishings, large mirrors, chandeliers, portraits, and fanciful murals that depicted sprites and fairies, mythological creatures, and kings and queens. As he walked through the entrance hall, he looked at the murals.

In some of them the royals and fairies were engaged in sports and games. In others, the fairies and kings led armies and celebrated victories. Still others showed life at court where enchantment went hand in hand with daily life.

The merchant walked on and found a banquet hall, a ballroom, and many large bedchambers with sitting rooms. Since it was already quite late and he was exhausted, the merchant chose one of the bedchambers and settled down to sleep.

CHAPTER 8

The Next Morning

The merchant tossed and turned all night. He dreamed of his children and his unhappy meeting with the lawyer.

After such a fitful night's sleep, the merchant was surprised to wake and find that it was already late the next morning. The sun was shining into the bedchamber where he slept.

Even though he wanted to meet and thank whoever lived at the castle, he hoped to get an early start to return home to his children before dark. He rose abruptly to prepare to leave.

"What is this?" the merchant asked when he reached for his clothes. Near the bed where he slept were a new suit of clothes and a pair of fine boots to replace his own dirty, tattered suit and shoes. He climbed out of bed and picked up the jacket and trousers that hung over the wardrobe. I must be in the home of a fairy that has taken pity on me, he thought as he dressed in the new clothes.

While dressing, he looked through a window and was able to see how magnificent the estate was. The snow and dark clouds of the previous evening had given way to blue skies and bright sun. Flower arbors and gardens with walking paths lined with orange trees stretched as far as he could see. This is amazing, he thought, taking it all in as he laced up the new boots.

Now more than ever he was convinced that he had come to a place that was under some kind of enchantment. He wondered about the murals he had seen the night before in the hallway.

He left the bedchamber. Passing the

mirror, he stopped to admire his reflection in his new suit of clothes. As he walked away from the mirror, he saw something else momentarily reflected there from the corner of his eye. "What was that?" he asked aloud, looking into the glass again. Convinced it was nothing, he walked on.

Surprisingly, he had no trouble finding his way through the labyrinth of apartments that led back to the great

hall and the small sitting room where he had dined the night before.

As if by magic, the table was set with a hot drink of cocoa and a light breakfast. "I can only thank you, my good fairies, for seeing to my needs again this morning," he said, raising his cup in a toast to the fairies in the mural and enjoying his meal.

CHAPTER 9

The Beast

After breakfast, the merchant went to the stable for his horse. On his way, he passed a rose garden and remembered Beauty's humble request. He selected a branch on which there were several perfect blooms and broke it off the bush. "My Beauty will enjoy these," he said to himself as he admired the flowers and their fine scent.

"What is the meaning of this?" came a ferocious voice from right behind him. Hovering menacingly near the merchant stood a horrible Beast. The merchant nearly fainted from the shock of seeing such a huge creature. The Beast resembled a man, stood upright, and was well dressed but, nonetheless, was a monster.

"How ungrateful you are, sir!" the Beast said in a frightful voice. "Is this the thanks I get for welcoming you into my castle and for saving your miserable life? You steal what I value most in the world! You'll pay for it, I assure you."

"Forgive me, Your Highness. I was taking a rose to one of my daughters," the merchant begged. He had fallen to the ground on his knees.

"Do not call me Your Highness. I do not want any important titles. I prefer to be called the Beast. Don't offer me false compliments, but just say what you think," he growled.

The merchant shook his head to acknowledge the Beast's words.

It took a few moments for the merchant to compose himself. Then he offered the Beast an honest explanation of why he wanted the rose.

"I meant no harm, sir. My dear daughter Beauty asked for nothing from my travels but a rose."

The Beast was curious about the girl and let the merchant continue.

"My other two daughters demanded things I could not hope to buy. You see, I lost my fortune and now I am penniless. I had traveled to town to see to my affairs, hoping to regain some small portion of my lost fortune," the weeping merchant continued.

The Beast listened with interest.

"Please, kind sir, spare me. I can see that you are fair and generous."

"You cannot flatter me," the Beast said, "but I will forgive you and let you go, on one condition."

"What is that?" the merchant asked in a low, humbled voice.

"One of your daughters must come here in your place. She must come of her own choosing and be willing to give her life in exchange for your own," the Beast demanded.

"I can't do that!" the merchant exclaimed.

"You must, if you are to live. If your daughters refuse, you must return within three months and accept your fate," the Beast commanded.

"But I—" the merchant began.

"There is nothing more to say! Go on and swear you will return in three months if none of your daughters come in your place," the Beast bellowed.

"I swear," the merchant said, but he had no intention of sending any of his children to suffer in his place at the hands of the monster.

"Don't think you can fool me, old man," the Beast roared. "If you don't return I will come for you! Do you promise to return?"

"I do," the merchant repeated sadly. He would take this opportunity to return home and say good-bye to his children. Then he would return to the castle and accept his fate.

"Take a rose to Beauty and leave whenever it pleases you," the Beast said, giving a branch with the loveliest rose to the merchant. "But don't leave before first returning to the chamber where you slept. There is a large empty chest there. Fill it with whatever treasures you want and I will send it to your home."

Then the Beast left the merchant, who stood shaking in the courtyard, frightened and bewildered.

CHAPTER 10

Treasures from the Castle

The merchant returned to the bed-chamber as quickly as he could, fearing that at any moment the Beast would be upon him again. He closed the door of the room behind him just to be safe. Inside he found the chest and began to gather fine things to put into it. The room was filled with precious objects of every kind. In fact, the closets and shelves were now laden with treasures for the taking!

"At least I will be able to leave something to my children," the merchant muttered halfheartedly as he filled the chest with gold, silver, and jewels.

The chest seemed to be bottomless.

No matter how much the merchant put into the chest, more fit into it. It seemed that it would be impossible for anyone to lift the chest. The merchant wondered if the Beast was mocking him and had no intention of sending the chest to his home.

Nonetheless, he filled it as much as possible. Then he left the bedchamber and quietly walked through the hall-ways, hoping to avoid the Beast again. Carrying the rose, he returned to the stable to get his horse, which had been prepared for riding. He mounted his horse and rode through the courtyard, passing the curious collection of statues once again.

As he rode down the tree-lined path, the merchant was filled with grief. The haven he had sought and luckily found out of the storm had turned into a nightmarish trap, threatening to destroy his family and all that he held most dear. Once again, fate had dealt him a terrible blow.

The horse seemed to know its way and found a road that led through the icy mist and swirling winds that obscured the castle. The horse was through the forest and home in a few short hours.

CHAPTER 11

A Bittersweet Reunion

Finally, the merchant came to the edge of the field where his sons were working.

"Hello, Father!" Henri shouted.

"What news have you from town?" Claude asked eagerly, wanting to know if they were rich once again.

The merchant signaled them to meet him back at the house. As the merchant rode toward the cottage, his two sons raced each other across the field to see who would get there first.

The merchant brought his horse to the stable. After removing the saddle, halter, and reins he went into the house, where his eager sons already stood.

Elise and Rene were lounging in the sitting room when they saw their father's approaching horse. They ran to the door to greet him, but only after they had messed their hair and smudged their faces with coal from the fireplace to make it appear that they had been hard at work.

"Father is back!" Rene shouted.

"Look at the fine clothes he wears!" Claude observed, assured that his father had returned with good news.

"Welcome home, Father," Henri said warmly.

"Let's see what he has brought us," Elise added excitedly.

Beauty, who was setting logs in the fireplace, was the first to give her dear father a welcoming hug. Her affection was most genuine.

The merchant hugged each of his children, grateful to have returned to them. Then, sadly, he held out the rose. "Here, Beauty, this is for you. The price

for it was very dear, indeed," he said, trying to hold back his tears.

"Father, what has happened?" Beauty asked, while her brothers helped the merchant into a chair.

"You will not believe what has befall-en me," said the merchant anxiously as his children listened.

First, the merchant told his children about the disappointing meeting with the lawyer.

"So we are no better off than before," Henri said, sighing.

"No, we are worse off than before," moaned Claude while Elise's and Rene's smiles turned to frowns.

"Let me continue," said the merchant. Then he told them about getting lost in the forest during the terrible storm and finding the castle.

"How lucky you were, Father, to find shelter on so horrible a night," said Elise while Rene nodded in agreement. In spite of their interruptions, the merchant went on. When he told them about meeting the Beast, they all gasped in horror.

"This is all your fault, Beauty!" Rene accused.

"How heartless you are not to even shed a tear," Elise added.

"It would never have happened if you hadn't asked for that ridiculous rose! Now that will be the death of our poor father," Rene hissed.

Claude and Henri stood by silently as their sisters tormented Beauty.

Beauty listened to their accusations, but didn't cry at all, even though she knew they were being unjust. Beauty knew what she had to do, and that was all that mattered to her.

CHAPTER 12

Beauty's Decision

"The reason I am not crying is because Father won't die on my behalf," Beauty said firmly. "The Beast has asked for one of his daughters, and I will go to save Father's life. That is how much I truly love him," Beauty said.

Beauty's brothers suddenly stepped forward. "No, Beauty, it is not you or Elise or Rene or Father who will return to the Beast's castle. *We* will go," Claude said bravely.

"Yes, Claude and I will go there and kill the Beast, or die in the effort!" exclaimed Henri courageously.

"Why should any of us suffer for Beauty's folly?" Rene asked while Elise shook her head in agreement.

"That is impossible, my sons," the merchant said, wringing his hands.

"Then one of us will go in your place," Claude proposed.

"Yes," said Henri again strongly.

"There is no way to outdo the Beast. He has powers you cannot begin to imagine," their father said. "He would only accept my promise of sending a daughter. I am old and have lived a long life. My only regret is not being able to spend the rest of my days with all of you. I will return to the castle in three months as I promised I would. I cannot accept Beauty's selfless offer, and I will not sacrifice my sons to the whims of this creature."

Beauty was deep in thought, overwhelmed by all that was happening. "Father," she said resolutely, "you may go to the castle. But you cannot stop me from following you there. I will accompany you one way or the other,

since it was my wish for a rose that put you in this dreadful situation."

Beauty's father and brothers tried to convince her to change her mind, but she would not listen to them. Only her sisters rejoiced at the thought of her imprisonment in the Beast's castle, since they were so jealous of her.

Later that evening when the merchant went into his bedroom, he saw the chest filled with treasures sent from the Beast's castle. Until that

moment, he had forgotten about it.

"The Beast has kept his word, and so I must keep mine when the time comes," he said sadly.

At first he decided not to tell his children about the chest because they would want to return to town if they thought they were again very rich. He wanted to remain in the country. He called Beauty into his room and entrusted her with his secret.

"Beauty, look at what the Beast sent home with me," he said, lifting handfuls of gold, silver coins, and gems from its depths. Beauty could not believe her eyes.

"We must keep this hidden from your brothers and sisters for the time being," he said.

Beauty told her father that gentlemen had been calling on Elise and Rene. She did not resent her sisters and truly wished them happiness. So she told her father that it would be best to let them have their fortunes and be married. The merchant saw the wisdom in this and agreed.

At the end of three months, Beauty and her father prepared for the journey to the Beast's castle. Rene and Elise had their fortunes and would soon be married, and her brothers would stay in the country for the time being.

Before parting from their sister, Elise and Rene rubbed their eyes with onions to fake tears. "Oh, dear sister, how we'll

miss you," Elise moaned dramatically.

"Be careful, dear Beauty," Rene said, sighing halfheartedly.

Beauty's brothers hugged her warmly and wished her and their father a safe journey and eventual return to their home.

Bravely, Beauty did not express sorrow at the thought of what her future held. She didn't want to add to her family's anxiety—or her own.

CHAPTER 13

Beauty Goes to the Beast's Castle

Beauty and her father left the farm and took the road toward town. After traveling for hours, the horses, which seemed to know the way, turned onto a path that led to the palace. As had happened before when the merchant was lost in the forest, they left the icy mist and swirling winds and entered a tree-lined path where flowers bloomed as if it were spring. In the distance, they could see the palace illuminated as if in anticipation of their arrival.

"What kind of place is this, Father?" Beauty asked.

"One of unbelievable enchantment, Beauty, and of an unknown future," the merchant said somberly as he led the way.

Beauty and her father dismounted from their horses. As they walked toward the palace they passed the statues that lined the courtyard. Beauty felt that the statues were watching her. Although the statues were clearly made of stone, their faces were eerily lifelike. Beauty shivered when she looked at them.

Beauty admired the lovely flower arbors as their horses went into the stable. Then Beauty's father led her

into the great hall.

Following her father, Beauty had just come into the hall and was passing the mirror when she turned to look into it. She saw a fleeting image there—as if someone else, a handsome young man, were passing the mirror with her and escorting her into the castle. She looked more closely. Seeing nothing, she thought she was just tired from the long trip. She rubbed her eyes and caught up with her father.

"Father, did you see...," she began to ask but he moved ahead quickly to go into the sitting room.

"Beauty, look at the table! Again it is set for a feast—this time for two," said the merchant. "I have no appetite, though," he added sadly as he sat down in one of the brocade chairs.

Strangely, Beauty was amused by this. The Beast intends to fatten me up before making a meal of me, she thought. Not wanting to upset her father more than he already was, she put the thought out of her head and prepared a plate for him and then one for herself.

"Surely this is meant for us," said Beauty as she took a seat at the table. They ate quietly until they heard a ferocious growl that echoed through the palace.

"This is the end, Beauty," said the merchant in tears, fearing the worst. "The Beast has come!"

The Beast's face and figure terrified

poor Beauty, but she tried not to show her feelings when he came and stood near her at the table.

"I am the Beast," he said harshly, introducing himself.

"I am Beauty," was her whispered response.

"Have you come of your own free will?" he asked Beauty.

"Yes, I have," she said, trembling as she uttered the words.

"And do you know that once your father leaves, you must stay here with me?" he questioned.

"Yes, it is my choice to do so," Beauty answered as calmly as she could.

The Beast seemed pleased with Beauty's response and moved toward the merchant's chair.

"Thank you, sir," the Beast said. "You are an honorable man. You must leave here tomorrow morning and never return. Before you leave, fill the chests in your bedchamber with whatever you

want to take back to your family in remembrance of Beauty. Good night, Beauty. Farewell, good man." The Beast abruptly left the room.

Beauty bowed her head and whispered, "Good night, Beast."

"Oh, Beauty!" the merchant cried when the Beast was gone. "You must not stay here! I can't leave you. You must go home and let me stay."

"No, Father, tomorrow morning you will leave and my fate will be in the hands of the Beast. Don't worry," Beauty assured him in a careful, determined tone. "I will be fine."

The merchant shook his head in resignation.

CHAPTER 14

A Sad Farewell

Beauty and her father dreaded the onset of night and the inevitable coming of morning that would separate them forever. For the rest of the day they tried to enjoy each other's company and remain cheerful, despite the heavy cloud that hung over them.

Beauty looked around the great hall. Like her father, she was captivated by the murals of magical fairies, mythological creatures, and royalty.

The Beast did not appear, and that helped put Beauty and her father more at ease.

Later that evening, Beauty helped her father fill the chests that were in

the same bedroom where he had slept during his first visit. At first, Beauty selected magnificent gowns, shoes, and hats for her sisters and fine suits, coats and boots for her brothers. But when her father opened a cabinet that was filled with gold and silver coins and jewels, she removed the clothing.

"Father," she said wisely, "it will be better for you to have coins that you can use readily. Then you can sell the jewels as you need to,"

"Yes, Beauty, that will be best," he agreed. But the more they put into the chest, the more room there was in it. So, in the end, Beauty was able to include the fine clothing with the coins and jewels after all.

"The Beast is again very generous," the merchant said, sure this time that he would find the chests when he returned home. It would be more than enough to live on for the rest of his life.

"Beauty, this is not worth the price of losing you to the Beast and an unknown future," the merchant said.

"Don't worry, Father, I am sure everything will work out for the best," Beauty said, not wanting to alarm him.

Then the merchant retired to go to sleep. Beauty selected another room and went quietly into it after bidding her father good night.

Once they were settled in their rooms and comfortable in their beds, they slept soundly, surprisingly so, for the entire night.

While Beauty slept, she dreamed. In her dream, a lady dressed in fine clothes appeared to her.

"Beauty, you have a good heart," the lady said. "By sacrificing your life to save your father's you have shown me a strong will, too. Your actions will be rewarded if you follow your heart."

The next morning when Beauty woke, she told her father about her dream and that the lady in it looked like one of the fairies in the murals in the great hall. Beauty was puzzled by the dream and its meaning.

"I hope your dream foretells good fortune," her father said, wishing the lady in Beauty's dream was the fairy he thought had seen to his needs during his first visit. Perhaps she would look after his daughter as well.

They walked arm in arm to the stable without encountering the Beast.

Once again, the merchant found his horse equipped with provisions, saddled, and ready for the journey home.

The merchant cried when he and his beloved Beauty finally had to part.

After watching her father ride down the courtyard path and disappear in the distance, Beauty returned to the great hall. At first she sat at the fireside table and cried. Although she had kept her true thoughts from her father, Beauty was certain that the Beast would devour her that night.

Mustering her courage, she decided to make the most of the time she had left and resolved to be strong. Then her thoughts turned to exploring the castle.

CHAPTER 15

Beauty's Room

Beauty discovered that the palace was filled with all kinds of wonders. The castle was very pleasant and warmly welcoming, in spite of its size, which stretched into two wings extended from the main building. She wandered through some of the grand rooms and then the smaller apartments.

She felt that it would take months for her to see all of its splendors, and wondered how much time she would have to explore it all.

In one part of the palace, she found an apartment with a sign over the door that read, "Beauty's Room."

Beauty approached the huge door.

To open it she had to take the great gilded knob in both hands and pull with all her strength. She was surprised to see the elegance of the rooms before her. The chamber contained a library with books on floor-to-ceiling shelves. The ceiling was vaulted with windows that let the sun's natural light fill the room. It was very comfortable and spacious. The library consisted of thousands of books, and she was eager to look over its contents.

Another room in the apartment contained many musical instruments, all of which she could play. Beauty noticed a harp, which was her favorite instrument since she could play it and sing at the same time. Unlike the one at home that she often played to the delight of her father and brothers, this one was made of gold and decorated with diamonds and rubies.

There is so much here to keep my mind off of my fate, Beauty thought. If

the Beast meant to harm me, then all of these amusements would not have been prepared for me, she reasoned. These thoughts gave her a renewed sense of comfort and courage.

Then Beauty went into the bedroom, where there was a large canopied bed with plush pillows. In the corner of the cozy room a warm fire welcomed her.

Picking up a book from the bedside table, she sat in a cushioned chair and opened the book to read. An inscription

written in gold said:

> *Welcome Beauty, abandon fear,*
> *You are queen and ruler here.*
> *Name your wishes, say your will,*
> *Each desire we will fulfill.*

Is it possible that this, too, is meant for me? Beauty wondered. Does the Beast have the power to read my mind and satisfy my wishes? It seems to be so.

Beauty held the book near her heart and thought about her future and how it would unfold at the Beast's castle.

CHAPTER 16

Visions

Puzzled by the words of the verse, Beauty wished more than anything that she could see her father. She turned toward the large mirror that stood near the dressing table and gasped. Reflected there was an image of her father just as he was returning home. Beauty's heart leaped with joy to see this image, but then it broke to see her father look so sad.

He greeted his children and handed the horse's reins to his sons. Elise and Rene tried to look concerned, but it was obvious that they were glad that Beauty had not returned with their father. Beauty blinked a tear from her eye. When she looked again at the mirror the vision was gone.

Beauty found some comfort in the Beast's willingness to please her with this vision.

Before lunch, Beauty had time to wander through more of the rooms of the palace. There was a sewing room with materials and ribbons of every color and fabric and tools for needlework and other crafts.

What lovely dresses I could make for

Elise and Rene, she thought to herself, holding up a bolt of colorful silk and a handful of pearl buttons. Or a warm coat for father and trousers for Claude and Henri, she mused, seeing supplies of wool fabric.

A loom stood in one corner of the room near a window that overlooked a lovely flower garden. Beauty noticed the loom and recalled her own modest loom at home and the joy she had felt weaving at it.

How strange that everything here seems made just to please me, she thought, remembering the verse from the book as she walked toward the loom.

Passing another mirror that was near the loom, she saw a wavering image. The harder she tried to perceive the image, the more difficult it became.

Finally, the image became steady enough for her to make out a handsome young man—the same man she had

seen on the evening of her arrival at the palace. He was standing near a majestic woman. Who are these phantoms? Beauty wondered.

The image faded quickly, and Beauty moved on in her explorations.

At noon, Beauty returned to the sitting room where she and her father had eaten breakfast. She was drawn there by the sound of music. Dinner was set upon the table. Beauty heard lovely music drifting through the room, but there were neither instruments nor musicians playing them.

How puzzling this is, she thought as she sat down to eat lunch. Remembering her father's belief that the palace was under an enchantment, she began to believe it herself.

CHAPTER 17

An Evening Together

Beauty returned to her apartment to rest. She fell asleep and dreamed of the handsome young man.

"Beauty," he said to her softly, "help me win my freedom."

When Beauty woke she could not make sense of the dream.

She had neither seen nor heard the Beast all day. It seemed that they were entirely alone at the palace—or were they? Who is the handsome young man? Where is he? she wondered. Perhaps he is being held against his will somewhere in the palace?

She rose from her nap to find the wardrobe in her room filled with lovely gowns, elegant shoes, and precious jewelry. Knowing they were meant for her, she selected a gown, dressed, and went to the main dining room for supper.

Then she heard a ferocious growl signaling the Beast's appearance. Although her spirits had lifted throughout the day as she viewed all of the splendors contained in the palace, Beauty's heart sank when she heard him approaching. Suddenly, she was afraid again.

"Beauty," the Beast asked, "can I

watch you while you dine?" He came closer to her chair.

"Yes if that is your wish," Beauty answered, trying to remain calm as she placed portions of the fine meal on her plate.

"You rule here, Beauty. You alone can permit me to stay or send me away if my appearance troubles you," the Beast continued. "I will leave with haste if you desire it. Do you find me to be ugly?" he asked bluntly.

"I cannot lie to you, Beast," Beauty said. "You are unbecoming, but you seem to be good-natured," she said, sensing now that he meant her no harm.

"Yes," the Beast said. "I am ugly. I am not well spoken or intelligent. I am a simple, dimwitted Beast."

"You may not be lovely to look at, Beast, but you have the gift of self-reflection," Beauty said. "That proves to me that you are neither simple nor dimwitted."

The Beast stood steadily beside

Beauty. "Enjoy your supper, Beauty," he said. "Know that everything in the palace is yours to enjoy and be amused by. If you are not happy here, I will be miserable."

"Beast, thank you for your kindness. Please don't be sad. Your ugliness seems insignificant in light of your gentle manner," Beauty said. She was grateful for the tenderness of his words and his concern for her happiness.

"Yes, I do have a good heart," the Beast said, "but I am still a hideous monster."

Beauty thought carefully about the Beast's words. "Beast" she said, "many men are pleasing to the eye, but brutal and more deserving of the name of Beast. "I prefer you to those whose good looks conceal a wicked heart," she said.

"If only I were clever enough to return a compliment for your kind words. I can only thank you plainly and offer my allegiance to you, Beauty," the Beast said, sighing, as Beauty finished her meal.

Beauty lowered her head. She was touched by the Beast's kindness and humility. She wished she could feel more comfortable in his presence.

As she learned more about him, she began to trust that she had nothing to fear, even if his looks still terrified her. With time, she hoped, his looks would no longer be a barrier to their growing friendship.

CHAPTER 18

The First Proposal

The more she got to know the Beast, the more comfortable Beauty felt in his presence. Although his appearance was frightening, he was kind, gentle, and generous. Each evening, the Beast asked her to tell him how she had spent her day, and they talked about the many things that she had encountered at the palace. Soon she learned that his tone, which was threatening and ferocious, was due to his awkward, bulky size and not his nature.

"Was everything to your liking?" the Beast would ask.

"Unbelievably so," Beauty would answer.

They would talk for some time longer. Beauty spoke of her life at home with her father, sisters, and brothers, while the Beast listened intently but without saying very much. The conversation was polite but not engaging. The Beast asked simple questions only, ones that required simple answers. That is, until he suddenly asked, "Will you marry me, Beauty?" Beauty nearly fainted.

"Answer yes or no without fear, as it pleases you," he added. Beauty worried that if she said no, in spite of his assurances, it would enrage the Beast or hurt him deeply. But Beauty was honest and courageous.

"No, Beast, I will not," she said plainly after a brief pause. She was afraid of what the Beast might do, but more so, she did not want to insult him after all he had done for her and her father.

"Argh-hhh-hhh!" The Beast sighed so loudly that the dreadful hiss echoed throughout the palace. Beauty sat still in her chair. She didn't know what to expect next. Her answer seemed to have wounded him terribly.

"Then good night to you, Beauty," the Beast said in a disheartened voice as he left the room. He turned to look at her a few times as he walked away.

"Poor Beast," Beauty whispered after a few moments. "How sad that a creature with such a good and generous nature should be so ugly."

CHAPTER 19

Encore

The next day Beauty rose early and continued to explore the palace. As she walked through the grand rooms, she discovered an aviary. It was a marvelous glass structure filled with hundreds of colorful birds of all sizes and kinds. From talking parrots and love birds to sparrows and hummingbirds, Beauty found the creatures to be as enchanting as their surroundings.

There were beautiful trees, bushes, shrubs, and birdhouses for them to live in. The birds sang joyful tunes. Beauty welcomed their happy chirping as a pleasant diversion to the hours she spent alone at the palace. In fact, the birds were so friendly that some of them landed on Beauty's hand when she extended it.

"How lovely to hear your pretty song," she said to the little birds that seemed to sing just for her. How nice it would be to have you closer to my chamber, she thought.

In the aviary, Beauty passed a looking glass. In it, she saw the handsome young man again. This time he extended his hand to her. A small bird was perched on his finger. She peered into the glass and reached out to touch the image, but it disappeared. Again she wondered who the stranger was and whether he needed her help.

Beauty left the aviary and went through another doorway. To her surprise, she was near her own apartment. The aviary and all of its wonderful singing birds were close to her room after all! Somehow, the Beast had provided for her happiness yet again. She was con-

fused by his actions but glad that he seemed to care about her happiness.

Beauty's curiosity compelled her to look for the young man. She decided to secretly try to find him while she explored the Beast's castle.

Tired from her long day, Beauty returned to her apartment. She lay down on her bed and drifted off to sleep. In her dream the young man appeared to her. Waking in time to dress for dinner, Beauty sat at the dressing table in her room. Looking in the mirror, she wished to see her father's image again, but it did not appear. She was becoming more concerned for him.

On her way to the dining hall that night, Beauty passed the portrait gallery. Among the pictures was a portrait of a king and beside it one of a queen. The elegant monarchs stared down at Beauty. What a surprise for Beauty when she realized that the queen in the picture and the woman whose image she

had seen in the mirror near the loom were the same person!

What does it all mean? she wondered. Then Beauty heard the horrible sound of the Beast approaching. Since she was still a little frightened of him, she quickly ran to the dining room.

The Beast joined her there and watched her dine just as he had done the night before.

"Beauty, will you marry me?" he asked again when she had finished.

"No, Beast, I cannot," Beauty answered sincerely, just as she had answered him the night before.

"Argh-hhh-hhh!" he cried pitifully, leaving the room. Beauty went to her bedchamber troubled by the Beast's deep sadness. She wondered how she could ease his suffering.

"I must find out who that young man is," Beauty whispered. "Perhaps he can tell me why the Beast is so sad and explain all of these puzzles."

Earlier, the magic mirror had shown that her sisters were to be married soon, and her brothers were well employed. Beauty's concern for her family had been eased somewhat, but she was deeply troubled by her father's sadness.

Tired from the day's adventures, and by her own anxieties, Beauty fell into a deep sleep.

CHAPTER 20

Time Passes

Day after day, Beauty explored the palace and its grounds. Night after night—always at nine o'clock—the Beast joined her. As Beauty talked, the Beast listened to her stories about when her family lived in the city and how their fortune had changed.

"Yes," the Beast said one night. "Our fates are unpredictable and often can be cruel."

As she spoke during those nighttime visits, it seemed to Beauty that the Beast was sullen and secretive. But she could never get him to speak more openly about himself. She was frustrated and felt sorry for him.

And each night, when the Beast asked her to marry him, Beauty always answered in the same way: "No, Beast, I cannot." Then, without fail, Beauty would hear the pathetic growl with which the Beast soothed his sorrow and signaled his departure for the evening.

As on the previous evenings, Beauty retired to her room after having rejected the Beast's proposal. As she slept, her mind was filled with images of times past

and present. Almost nightly the kind fairy appeared to her in her dreams.

"Beauty, follow your heart," the fairy always advised.

In Beauty's dreams, encounters with the Beast mixed with visions of the handsome young man.

Beauty still had not found out much about the young man, but he was constantly in her dreams and in her thoughts. Now the handsome face of the young man appeared to her more often and at the oddest moments, while she was awake and asleep.

Although Beauty was nearly certain that the Beast meant her no harm, she was afraid to ask him about the young man. Could the Beast be holding him captive, she wondered.

CHAPTER 21

Shadows in the Moonlight

Each day new surprises unfolded to lift Beauty's spirits, but her curiosity about the handsome young man was never satisfied. Perhaps there was no answer to this puzzle, she thought.

One night before retiring, Beauty walked in the rose garden in the moonlight. The arbors were filled with sweet-smelling blossoms of every color. It concerned her that the Beast cared for her so much and that she did not care for him in the same way.

While lost in her thoughts, Beauty came upon a magnificently decorated gazebo with beautiful flowering plants. It stood in the center of the garden.

Mirrored panels etched with roses separated each section of the glass walls. When she entered the gazebo, the images on the mirrors startled her. There she was, reflected back in the many mirrors, and by her side was the mysterious young man!

"Who are you?" she asked, determined to find an answer.

"Argh-hhh-hhh!" a cry rang out from a high turret in the castle. Glancing up,

Beauty saw the Beast's massive shadow in the window. She was more confused than ever.

The wavering image in the mirror faded. Shaken, Beauty went to her room and finally fell asleep. In her dreams, the fine lady appeared to her again.

"Beauty, follow your heart and you will be rewarded with true happiness," the kind fairy whispered. Then the fairy vanished, and Beauty dreamed of the handsome young man.

"Beauty, don't be swayed by appearances," he begged. Beauty woke with a start. Although the sun had risen, her mind was still clouded.

CHAPTER 22

The Magical Theater

Since the Beast only visited her briefly each evening, Beauty was alone most of the time. Whenever she was lonely, she would think of a diversion and it was magically supplied. One day she found a special room. It was the most amazing marvel yet discovered at the palace, and in it she encountered the most incredible vision of all.

This special room was a theater. It was quite dark and had many draped windows. There were many chairs standing vacant, ready for an audience. Golden candelabra lined the walls. They lit themselves as she entered. Whenever she sat at one of the chairs, the lights dimmed and the curtain she sat before rolled up. Then she would see a live stage play, an opera or a comedy. Whatever was her wish would appear to her.

Beauty spent much of her time in this room to pass the hours of each day while she waited for dinnertime and the Beast's visit.

One day, a drama unfolded in which the Beast and the handsome young man quarreled over who would be king, and each beckoned Beauty to choose between them! Beauty was so disturbed by the image that she rose from her chair, causing the drama to end abruptly.

Afterward she wished she hadn't acted so impulsively. She often returned to the theater to see if that same drama would appear. Perhaps it could give her answers to her many questions, she thought, but it never did.

With so many diversions, time passed quickly, and soon Beauty realized that

she had been at the castle for more than three months.

Although he was not witty, the Beast had many fine qualities. Beauty no longer dreaded his visits, but welcomed them. Only two things weighed on her conscience. The first was the Beast's proposals, which he made every night without fail. The second was that although she was very happy at the palace, she still wondered if the handsome young man was being held prisoner by the Beast.

Finally, one night Beauty asked, "Beast, are we alone at the palace?"

"Yes, Beauty, we are alone here," he assured her.

Beauty accepted his answer and finished her meal. Then the Beast proposed to her again.

This time, Beauty responded, "I cannot consent to marry you and I cannot deceive you about my heart's intentions. I will always be your friend. Can

134

you be satisfied with that?"

"If I *must* be satisfied, I will be satisfied. I know I can't expect more. I love you, Beauty, and I can be happy if you stay with me always. Promise that you'll never leave me," he begged.

Beauty felt that she could now make that promise. She was quite happy with the Beast at the palace. He saw to her every need, and it was due to his generosity that her family once again prospered. All but one of her desires were met there. Beauty longed to see her father again. Lately, whenever she peered into the mirror in her room, she could see that he was unhappy. "If he knew that I am well and content, he would be happy again," she murmured.

CHAPTER 23

Beauty's Request

"Beast," Beauty said, "I will promise never to leave you, but I must see my father again. He needs me. I will die of worry if I can't see him again."

"I would rather die myself than cause you harm," the Beast sighed.

"Will you allow me to go to him then?" she asked.

"I will send you to your father, Beauty. You can stay with him, and in so doing I will die of grief for losing you," he wailed.

Beauty looked tenderly at the Beast. "Beast, I promise to return in one week if you permit me to go. You have already shown me through the mirror that my sisters are married and that my brothers have gone into the king's service. Just let me spend a week with my dear father. He is all alone and not well. I will willingly return to you then," Beauty pleaded. "It has been so long since I have seen him, and he needs me."

"Do you promise to return after one week?" the Beast asked.

Beauty was alarmed by the desperate look in his eyes. "Yes," she answered sincerely.

"Then you can go. You will be there in the morning," the Beast said. "When you are ready to return, turn your ring around on your finger before going to sleep and say, 'I wish to return to my Beast.' Farewell, Beauty," he said. His sigh rattled the walls.

That night Beauty was very distressed for having caused the Beast to grieve so deeply. She also dreamed again of the handsome young man.

"Beauty how can you abandon me?" he asked.

Beauty awoke abruptly.

Troubled by the dream, and concerned about the Beast, Beauty knew what she had to do. She was determined to make her visit and return as soon as she was sure of her father's well-being.

After that, she slept peacefully, trusting that all would be well.

CHAPTER 24

A Family Reunion

Beauty woke late the next morning. As the sun streamed through a small circular window, she looked around, a bit bewildered, before recognizing that now she was in her loft room at her father's cottage in the country. Silently, she thanked the Beast.

How good is my Beast that he has seen to my happiness yet again and made this wish above all others come true? she marveled.

The room was now finely furnished, and the country house had been repaired due to the treasure her father had gotten from the Beast. Beauty rang the little bell that was on the bedside table. A maid entered and nearly fainted at seeing her standing in a robe and slippers in the middle of the room.

"What is it, Jeannette?" asked the merchant running up to the loft to see what had happened.

"Beauty, you have returned!" he exclaimed, hugging his daughter. "But how—?"

"The Beast allowed it, but I must return to the palace in one week, Father," Beauty said. "I promised him that I would return to him. He is so good to me," she said.

"Yes, when it is time, but for now let me look at you!" rejoiced her father.

So happy were father and daughter in their reunion that they smiled and hugged each other for a long time. Then the merchant told Beauty how, with the riches sent by the Beast, he was able to become a prosperous merchant again. Beauty told him of the good times she had experienced at the Beast's palace.

"Father, there is such enchantment there. More than you can imagine," Beauty continued, telling him about the marvels she discovered there and about the handsome young man.

"I do not know what it all means," the merchant said. "Perhaps there is no answer, only your imagination conjuring the image, and he is not a prisoner of the palace but a prisoner of *your* dreams," he proposed.

"I wonder too, Father," she said thoughtfully.

"Sir, there is a trunk in the next room," the maid declared, interrupting their reunion. A trunk filled with gowns embellished with gold, diamonds, and jewels of every type was in the next room. Beauty thanked the Beast again for this sign of his affection for her. She chose a gown to wear and put aside the remaining dresses for her sisters.

"Elise and Rene will look lovely in these," she said to her father. As she

said these words, the trunk and gowns disappeared!

"Beauty, it seems that the Beast wants you to keep these for yourself," her father said. Then the gowns and the trunk reappeared.

"You must be right, Father," Beauty agreed, laughing gaily at this latest enchantment.

While Beauty dressed, her father spread the news of her return. When the horse-drawn coaches carrying her sisters and their husbands arrived, Beauty went downstairs to the parlor to greet them.

Soon Beauty's whole family surrounded her. Her brothers were there on leave from the king's service for a short time. They joyously gave her great bear hugs, while her sisters expressed their astonishment.

"We thought you were lost for sure," Elise said. "How happy we are that you have returned to us." Her eyes were fixed on the jeweled choker around Beauty's neck.

Rene nodded her head, admiring the lovely gown that Beauty wore.

The gown was made of the most extraordinary silk and satin materials. Pearls were embroidered along the neckline. The dress had a short train so that Beauty looked like a princess wearing it. In truth, it was the most simple of the gowns in the trunk, but it was the perfect complement to Beauty's natural loveliness.

Beauty welcomed her sisters and their husbands with open arms and hugs of genuine affection. Her own happiness was obvious and her love for her sisters unconditional. Elise and Rene were more jealous than ever of Beauty.

Elise whispered to Rene, "She seems so happy."

"And here we are," Rene whispered back, "stuck with miserable husbands."

"It isn't fair," they said in unison.

Elise had married a man who was very good looking but so conceited that he cared only about his own needs and desires. Rene had married a very clever man, but he was stingy and mean. His constant criticisms tortured Rene, and they quarreled all of the time.

Now their husbands were fawning over Beauty!

Beauty told everyone about the magical palace and the generous Beast. She assured them that she was happy.

The Beast saw to her every need. She told them that her promise to return was truly her wish and not just in gratitude for all the Beast had done for her and her family.

Elise and Rene were enraged by Beauty's good fortune and were determined to make her miserable.

CHAPTER 25

Envy Everlasting

E lise and Rene left the parlor to take a breath of fresh air alone in the garden.

"How unimaginable it is to me that our wretched little sister should be so happy!" Rene complained as she wiped a tear from her eyes.

"How can she be the one to look so beautiful and content after all we've been through?" Elise hissed through clenched teeth. "We must not let her return to the Beast."

"Yes, Elise. Then the Beast will become so angry that he'll devour her for breaking her word," Rene conspired.

Elise and Rene pretended to be

crushed by the thought of Beauty leaving the family again.

"Oh, dear sister," Rene pleaded, "you *must* stay with us. Father needs you. Without you, he will die."

"Beauty, it is our dream come true that our little sister has returned home and is safe. Stay with us," Elise added.

Elise and Rene were so kind to their younger sister that Beauty was overjoyed at their change of heart. They made such a fuss over the prospect of her leaving

them that they cried uncontrollably and tore at their hair.

"Father will simply die if you leave again," Elise said.

"Yes," Rene agreed, "his heart will surely break."

Torn between causing the Beast's death and her father's, Beauty did not know what to do. She was tormented, but hoped that if she stayed home a little while longer, she could convince her family that she would be safe at the palace.

CHAPTER 26

The Dream

Many nights after the week's deadline had past, Beauty dreamed that she was in the palace rose garden. The Beast was lying on the grass near a pond. His breathing was strained and he seemed to be in pain. He whispered, "Beauty, why have you not returned to me?"

The dream faded, and another one took its place. In this dream, the kind fairy appeared to her. "Beauty, you have broken your promise. The Beast is dying," the fairy said sadly.

"No!" Beauty called out, waking from the dream with a start. She sat up and began to cry. At that moment, she realized that she loved the Beast. The vision

of the handsome young man was probably nothing more than that—a fleeting image. The Beast had said that they were alone, so perhaps her father was right. After all, during her stay with her family Beauty had not dreamed of the young man at all.

How wicked of me to break my promise to my Beast, she thought. He was so kind and thoughtful. I should not have refused to marry him. I know now that I would be happy with him. I could never forgive myself if he suffered or died because of me.

She turned the ring on her finger and said, "I want to return to my Beast."

Beauty fell back to sleep, and when she woke she was at the Beast's palace.

CHAPTER 27

Searching for the Beast

"I am back!" Beauty cried out with joy when she saw that she was at the palace. She dressed in a hurry and went to look for the Beast. It was early morning. She couldn't find him anywhere. Since he never walked about the palace during the day, she thought, he'll come in the evening while I dine, as he always does.

Beauty spent the day in her usual activities but anxiously awaited the Beast's arrival at nine o'clock. The hours at the palace never passed so slowly as they did that day.

She went into the aviary to enjoy the birds' happy songs, but their melodies were sad.

She went into the music room to play the harp, but the tune was melancholy and did not entertain her.

She went to the library to read a favorite book, but couldn't concentrate on the story.

She went to the theater room, which always lifted her spirits, but this time the show did not interest her.

At the gazebo Beauty found that even the flowers seemed wilted.

Finally, it was time for dinner. Beauty

dressed in one of the best gowns she could find and went to the banquet hall. The clock struck nine, but the Beast did not come to talk with her.

"Oh, where is my Beast?" Beauty wailed, giving in to the emotions that had clouded her mind and heart throughout the long and wearying day.

Beauty's dream flashed through her mind. She was afraid that the Beast was dead. She ran from room to room in the palace, searching for him. "Beast, Beast, where are you?" she called out. Worrying about the Beast consumed her every thought.

Wringing her hands in despair, her hopes ever sinking, Beauty recalled that in her dream she had seen the Beast lying on the grass near a pond in the garden. She ran there as quickly as she could.

There he was, his huge body sprawled on the ground. His breath was short and choked. He was barely conscious when she bent down to feel his pulse. Even though his pulse was weak, she could feel the faint beating of his heart. She drew water from the pond and gently splashed his face with it.

"You broke your promise," the Beast whispered.

"My poor Beast," Beauty cried, tenderly holding his hand in hers.

"When you didn't return, I could not eat or sleep," the Beast moaned.

"Beast, you must not die!" Beauty

said. "I cannot live without you. I love you, Beast. I will marry you!"

Gently, Beauty kissed his cheek. Brilliant lights and fireworks went off above the palace. Cannons blasted into the air, and music swelled around them.

The statues in the courtyard and throughout the palace suddenly came to life. A golden chariot drawn by a unicorn emerged from the mist that surrounded the palace. Beauty hardly noticed any of this. Her only concern was for the Beast's well-being.

CHAPTER 28

No Longer a Beast

Wiping the tears from her eyes, Beauty looked at the Beast. But the Beast was gone! In his place was the handsome young man!

"Who *are* you?" Beauty asked. "And where is my Beast?"

"Beauty, I am the Beast. Your love has broken the spell under which I have lived for years, alone and in pain. Your friendship and companionship restored my hope that I would rule here as a prince, and no longer as a Beast. But when you left, all of my hopes died. I wanted to die, too."

The sound of the unicorn drew their attention to the chariot that had appeared in the garden. Two women stepped from it. Both were dressed in fine clothing. Beauty recognized one as the kind fairy in her dreams. The other woman wore a crown and a royal robe. Beauty recognized her from the portrait in the gallery.

"Well, Your Majesty," the fairy said as she and the queen approached the happy young couple, "here is Beauty, the only young woman who could break the spell that doomed your son to live in the form of a beast. You will never find a more loving, caring, and devoted daughter-in-law."

Beauty curtsied before the queen, who stepped forward and took Beauty's hands in both of hers.

"Thank you, Beauty, for all you have done to restore my son and his kingdom," the queen exclaimed.

Then the queen placed her arms around the prince and hugged him with such happiness and joy that, once

again, fireworks and cannons went off around the palace. The people who had been statues danced merrily.

"You see, Beauty," said the kind fairy, "all that exists here was created to protect the prince until he could be restored to his human form."

Beauty was amazed and thrilled to discover that her Beast and the handsome young man were one and the same being.

"Beauty, because of the enchantment

I was not able to reveal my identity to you. I could only let you see my true self in the reflections cast by mirrors and in your dreams."

"Those images confused me and nearly led my heart astray," Beauty said lovingly. "How long have you suffered?" she asked the prince.

"I can hardly remember now how long it has been," the prince said. He took Beauty's hand as they sat in the rose garden. "It seems like forever. Before you came, I had no hope."

CHAPTER 29

The Evil Fairy

"My story begins when an evil fairy sought to increase her power and control my destiny. It was this fairy who caused my transformation from man to Beast.

"In my youth the alliance between mortals and fairies was strong," the prince explained. "The murals in the great hall depict a time when fairies and kings were allies who helped one another against invading armies, imps, ogres, witches and sorcerers."

Beauty remembered the murals that had captivated her when she first arrived at the palace.

"Each envied the other's power,

though," the kind fairy said. "Some fairies believed our mystical abilities outweighed worldly matters and made us superior to men, and the king—the most sovereign ruler of all the land, who answered to no one but the divine— would never concede to such a thing."

Beauty listened to the incredible tale. Could this be true? she thought.

"One such powerful fairy was a confidante to my father, the king. She was both feared and loved," the prince said.

"Mostly feared," the queen added, "since she was unpredictable and was known to take offense easily—often taking merciless vengeance on the offender."

"When my father died, this fairy helped my mother raise me. Wise men of the court advised it so as not to anger the fairy. She was charged with my education and keeping me safe from harm. This she did, but in so doing her own ambitions and desire for control overcame her. In my father's untimely death, which elevated me as his heir to the kingdom, she saw her opportunity." ·

"Yes," the queen said, taking her son's arm affectionately. "She cared for the prince while I was defending his kingdom against a neighboring army."

"As I grew older and wanted to assist my mother in the campaign to protect my kingdom," the prince continued, "the fairy refused to let me join my mother on the battlefield. When, at last, my mother returned in triumph years later, the fairy approached her with the plan she had devised ever since my father's death."

The prince, the queen, and the kind fairy recalled the events that led to that horrible, fateful day when all the prince-turned-beast could do was wait...and wait....

CHAPTER 30

Reliving the Past

"Good Queen, welcome home. Here is your son," said the evil fairy, presenting the prince.

The queen had not been to the palace in quite a while. It had been the king's summer retreat. The queen chose it for her homecoming after the war to rest and regain her strength and peace of mind.

"Thank you for all you have done to keep my son safe," the queen said. "How can I ever repay you?"

The question, so innocently asked, was what the evil fairy wanted to hear.

"My Queen, now that you have returned and your son's kingdom is secure, I demand that you let us marry. I will be his wife, and as a queen with magical powers, I will protect his safety and prosperity," she stated boldly.

Without a moment's hesitation, the queen cried, "Are you mad?"

The prince, too, thought the fairy's demand was an unbelievable one. He wanted to marry someone of his own choosing and someone he loved.

"Why is it absurd, madam?" the fairy questioned. "There would be no more powerful kingdom on earth than your son's if he were to marry me."

The queen merely raised her head and, looking by chance into the great mirror, said, "Can you not see for yourself why?" she asked.

The prince's gentle reflection stood in sharp contrast to the hard, spiteful countenance of the fairy, whose rage was growing.

"I lower myself to marry a mere mortal, when I could choose from the most powerful genies in the universe," she cried. "You should be honored at my proposal! What do you say, young prince? Do you refuse to marry me?"

"Yes, I refuse to marry you," he answered. "We can repay you some other way."

"Insignificant vain mortals! You shall pay for your insolence!" she said, striking the prince.

Overcome by the shock of the blow, the prince fell to the ground. He tried

to rise but couldn't. He was so heavy, he could only lift himself a few inches from the ground. His hands were now huge paws. His body had been transformed into that of a massive beast!

"Now find someone more to your liking!" the evil fairy laughed. "Without your title, without your good looks, without your wit or charm, see if you can find someone to love you. Until you do, you will remain in the hideous form of a dim-witted beast. And should you dare to tell anyone what has happened here, you will be doomed forevermore!" Then she disappeared.

The prince-turned-beast and his mother were devastated, until a gentle voice reassuringly called out: "Take courage! It will take time, but hope and love can change one's destiny."

Fortunately, the kind fairy was in the great hall at the time.

"Can you help us?" the queen asked.

"Perhaps," the fairy answered. "By meeting the condition of the spell it could be broken. I will find a girl whose heart is true," she promised.

"What about the people who have seen the transformation?" the queen asked with concern.

"I will cast a spell over everyone at the palace to keep them frozen in time until the evil spell is broken."

The prince and the queen agreed.

"But you must be careful," she cautioned the prince. "Keep your secret. Your power of speech will be your undoing if you reveal what has happened to you. That is why the wicked fairy changed only your form, and not your abilities."

Then the kind fairy waved her wand and said a few magic words. Everyone at the summer palace except the queen, the Beast, and the kind fairy, turned to stone, and a heavy mist rose up around the estate to keep passersby away.

The Beast kept himself secluded at the palace. Occasionally, the fairy visited the Beast to let him know of her progress in finding a solution.

The weeks turned into months, then years. His one comfort was seeing the many wonders at the palace. He especially loved the rose garden that he cultivated. It was these beloved roses that had finally brought Beauty to him.

It seemed that the Beast's waiting was over when the merchant became lost in the woods. When he heard about the merchant's kind-hearted daughter, the Beast began to hope once again. And then the good fairy's plan began to unfold. . . .

CHAPTER 31

A Wedding at the Great Hall

"Beauty," the fairy said, "your willingness to sacrifice your own life to save your father's proved that you were truly capable of the kind of love and devotion that was needed to free the prince."

"Beauty," said the prince, "you—*only you*—accepted me because you saw that underneath my physical appearance, I had a generous, gentle heart that would love and protect you always."

After the tale was told, they were all magically transported into the castle. As they walked down the great hall, they passed the gilded mirror. Beauty peered into it. This time, she saw only the reflection cast by a couple happily walking arm in arm toward their wedding. There were no mysterious visions of the past or unwelcome images.

To Beauty's surprise, her whole family was in the great hall. They had been brought there by the good fairy's magic to celebrate the happy event.

"True happiness is your reward, Beauty," the fairy said, "for being wise and choosing virtue over good looks and wit. You have found a person in whom all those qualities exist. I know becoming queen will never change your true heart."

Beauty's father was overwhelmed with happiness for his daughter. Her brothers were thrilled by her good fortune.

Only Elise and Rene sneered at her from a corner of the great hall. They were furious at how Beauty's situation with the Beast had turned out.

"Ladies," the fairy said, "your hearts

are filled with anger and jealousy. To
match your hearts of stone, you shall
both become statues guarding the doors
of your sister's palace. But beneath the
stone you will keep your sense of reason
so that you can always reflect on the
faults that led to your transformation.
Perhaps in time you will repent."

Elise and Rene could not answer the
fairy, for they were frozen by fear.

"Wait, dear fairy," Beauty called out.
"Please do not harm my sisters. In

time, I am sure they will change," she said lovingly, not wanting them to suffer the kind of fate her beloved Beast had endured.

"Most human faults can be changed in time," the fairy answered her. "But the faults of your sisters—hatred and envy—are almost impossible to alter. Still, I will grant your wish. Maybe your goodness will rub off on them after all. Stranger things have happened."

Beauty couldn't agree more. Surely, stranger things *had* happened!

With a stroke of her wand, the fairy transformed the hall into a wedding banquet. Beauty and her beloved prince were married, to the great joy of their families and their subjects. Afterward, they returned to the official palace.

But Beauty and the prince loved the enchantments at the summer palace, and they wanted to live there.

"Now that the spell is broken," the kind fairy said, "you both must accept your responsibilities. But you can visit the summer palace whenever you wish. I will always ensure that the magic there endures to delight you both."

And it did.

Epilogue

Beauty and the prince were grateful for the good fairy's favors. Whenever they wanted to return to the summer palace, they only had to summon the unicorn that led the golden chariot, an enchanted wedding gift from the kind fairy. It would appear in a flash and transport them to the castle in the blink of an eye.

Beauty and the prince visited the palace often to enjoy the gazebo, the theater room, and all of the other splendors there. They spent most of their time enjoying the rose garden and its lovely flowers, which were a symbol of their deep love and eternal happiness.

Although they were mortal, their time on earth seemed to be an endless enchantment that enabled them to truly live happily every after.

About the Author

Jeanne-Marie le Prince was born in Rouen, France, in 1711. In 1743, she married a man named Beaumont. The marriage lasted only two years, but she kept her husband's last name.

In 1746, Beaumont moved to England. There she wrote novels and short stories based on her work as a governess and tutor. In 1748, her first novel was published in France.

In 1756, she wrote her own version of "Beauty and the Beast." The original story by Madame Gabrielle de Villaneuve had been written for adults. Beaumont's version was aimed at a younger audience.

Beaumont wrote more than seventy books, fairy tales, and short stories. Her emphasis on selfless love and happy endings has influenced fairy tale literature for more than three centuries. She died in 1780.

Treasury of Illustrated Classics

Adventures of Huckleberry Finn
The Adventures of Pinocchio
The Adventures of Robin Hood
The Adventures of Sherlock Holmes
The Adventures of Tom Sawyer
Alice in Wonderland
Anne of Green Gables
Beauty and the Beast
Black Beauty
The Call of the Wild
Frankenstein
Great Expectations
Gulliver's Travels
Heidi
Jane Eyre
Journey to the Center of the Earth
The Jungle Book
King Arthur and the Knights of the Round Table
The Legend of Sleepy Hollow & Rip Van Winkle
A Little Princess
Little Women
Moby Dick
Oliver Twist
Peter Pan
The Prince and the Pauper
Pygmalion
Rebecca of Sunnybrook Farm
Robinson Crusoe
The Secret Garden
Swiss Family Robinson
The Time Machine
Treasure Island
20,000 Leagues Under the Sea
White Fang
The Wind in the Willows
The Wizard of Oz